Island
~ of ~
Sodor

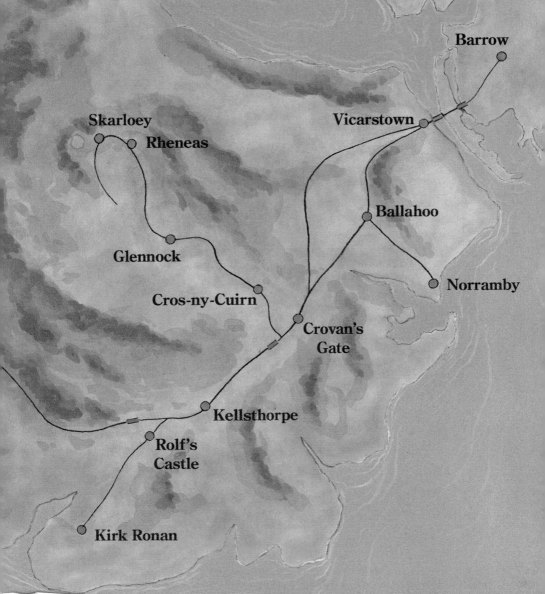

Barrow

Skarloey

Rheneas

Vicarstown

Ballahoo

Glennock

Cros-ny-Cuirn

Norramby

Crovan's
Gate

Kellsthorpe

Rolf's
Castle

Kirk Ronan

Thomas the Tank Engine & Friends™

CREATED BY BRITT ALLCROFT

Original holiday story based on The Railway Series by The Reverend W Awdry.
© 2008 Gullane (Thomas) LLC.
Thomas the Tank Engine & Friends and Thomas & Friends are trademarks of
Gullane (Thomas) Limited. Thomas the Tank Engine & Friends & Design is Reg.
U.S. Pat. & Tm. Off. HIT and the HIT Entertainment logo are trademarks of HIT
Entertainment Limited.

www.randomhouse.com/kids/thomas
www.thomasandfriends.com

Library of Congress Cataloging-in-Publication Data
Valentine's Day in Vicarstown / illustrated by Richard Courtney.
  p. cm.
"Thomas the Tank Engine & Friends created by Britt Allcroft, based on
The Railway Series by The Reverend W Awdry."
Summary: Percy the train engine is excited about the Valentine's Day party, but
a blizzard makes it difficult to get there.
ISBN 978-0-375-84755-4
[1. Railroad trains—Fiction. 2. Valentine's Day—Fiction.]
I. Awdry, W. Railway series. II. Title.
PZ7.C83166 Val 2008   [E]—dc22   2008028342

MANUFACTURED IN CHINA
10 9 8 7 6 5 4

HiT entertainment

Valentine's Day in Vicarstown

Based on The Railway Series
by The Reverend W Awdry

Illustrated by Richard Courtney

RANDOM HOUSE 🏠 NEW YORK

It was a cold, clear February morning, and Percy was tired. He had worked hard all night to deliver the mail and was ready to rest in the Shed.

Thomas was just leaving as Percy chugged into the Yard. "Hello, Percy," he peeped. "I hope you had a good night with the mail run."

"It was cold," replied Percy. "But I was—"

"Sorry, Percy, but I must go," interrupted
Thomas. "I am supposed to be working at the
Docks for a couple of days. Will you tell me about
it at the Valentine's Day party? *Peep, peep!*"

Percy rolled up to Edward.
"Edward, I forgot about the Valentine's Day party. What happens there?" Percy asked.

Edward smiled. "Every Valentine's Day, there is a big party at the station in Vicarstown. The children come and exchange valentine cards and sing songs. Sometimes they give valentines to their favorite engines."

Percy hoped he would get some valentines.

All day, Percy asked the other engines about the Valentine's Day party.

"Last year," said James, "I received twelve valentines."

"Bah! I am too important to think about valentines," rumbled Gordon.

The next morning, Percy was heading home from the mail run. It was very dark and windy, and he noticed that it wasn't getting lighter. Where was the sun? The clouds were dark and snow was starting to fall. It began as a light snow, but the wind blew harder and harder, and the snow came down faster and faster.

Percy could barely see where he was going.
The snow drifted across the tracks, and it
was very hard to move. He had to get back to
the Yard!

After a long time, Percy finally made it.
The larger engines that had snowplows had been
sent out to try to keep the tracks clear, but Percy
stayed in the Shed and watched the snow
continue to fall. And fall. And fall.

The next morning, Sir Topham Hatt came to the Yard. He was so bundled up, he could barely move.

"Percy, Thomas is snowed in at Brendam. Everyone is going to have to be extra Really Useful. Maybe Thomas' snowplow will fit you. . . ."

The next few days were very busy. Percy
struggled with Thomas' snowplow, which was a
little too big, but he still managed to clear most of
the Branch Line all by himself. He helped Terence
clear snow from the Yard, and at night he still
had to deliver the mail.

Before he knew it, it was time to go to
Vicarstown for the big Valentine's Day party.

Vicarstown is a large town on the east coast of Sodor. The station is big and there are many platforms. Percy hoped that the tracks were clear enough for Thomas to get there. The station had been decorated with hearts and red streamers. And at the front of each platform was a little mailbox.

"More mail?" asked Percy. "Am I going to have to miss the party?"

His Driver laughed. "No, Percy. Those are boxes for valentines."

The party started to get crowded. Lots of children ran up to say hello to Percy. He was very nice to them, but he was still looking for Thomas. He saw Edward arrive and then Emily. He saw children exchanging valentine cards and laughing and having a wonderful time.

He even saw some children putting small
envelopes into his valentine mailbox!
And then the crowd got suddenly quiet.

Sir Topham Hatt made an announcement. "Thank you for coming to this splendid party. And to my engines, you are all my Really Useful valentines. For your hard work cleaning up after the blizzard, each of you will get a hopper full of high-grade coal," he promised. "And a good washing at the Works as soon as it warms up."

Everyone cheered and applauded.

Then some of the children got together and sang songs. After the singing, everyone exchanged valentine cards, and the children received fruits and chocolate hearts and other valentine treats.

At long last, Thomas pulled up next to Percy.
The children crowded around Thomas and
Percy, smiling and showing the engines all
their valentine cards. They counted Thomas'
valentines. Thomas had twenty!

Then they started counting Percy's.

"... eighteen ... nineteen ... twenty ..."

"... twenty-one! The most of all!" peeped Percy.

"That last one was from me," said Sir Topham Hatt. "You have made yourself extra useful this week." He continued, "Percy has gotten pretty handy with your snowplow, Thomas."

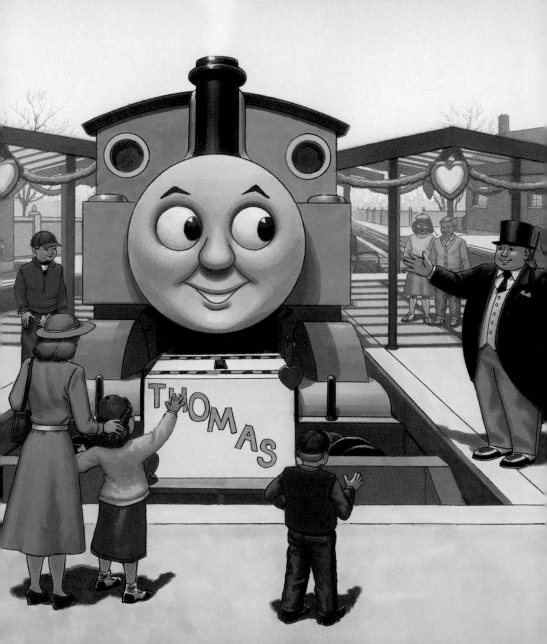

"He can have it!" laughed Thomas. "Less plowing for me!"

Percy smiled. He was glad to have a best friend like Thomas.

Can you find these things in the pictures of this story?